Hi,

Sam Kerr here, captain of the Matildas and striker for Chelsea FC.

I hope you have enjoyed *The Flip Out* and *A New Knight*, the first two books in my new series, which tells how I took up playing soccer after I wasn't allowed to play AFL anymore, and how, after a rough start, I have settled into playing soccer for the Knights. But there is still so much to learn!

The *Kicking Goals* series follows my story from a soccer newbie to a skilled striker. In these books, I share my experiences and challenges on and off the pitch, and I can't wait to share my journey with you.

I hope you love them as much as I do!

Sam

D1642844

SAM KERR: KICKING GOALS: SPORTS DAY
First published in Australia in 2022 by
Simon & Schuster (Australia) Pty Limited
Suite 19A, Level 1, Building C, 450 Miller Street, Cammeray, NSW 2062

10 9 8 7 6 5 4 3 2 1

Sydney New York London Toronto New Delhi
Visit our website at www.simonandschuster.com.au

© Sam Kerr and Fiona Harris 2022

All rights reserved. No part of this publication may be reproduced, stored in a
retrieval system, or transmitted in any form or by any means, electronic, mechanical,
photocopying, recording or otherwise, without prior permission of the publisher.

A catalogue record for this
book is available from the
National Library of Australia

ISBN: 9781761100918

Cover design: Meng Koach
Cover and internal images: Aki Fukuoka
Photo of Sam Kerr: Football Australia
Typeset by Midland Typesetters, Australia
Printed and bound in Australia by Griffin Press

The paper this book is printed on is certified against the
Forest Stewardship Council® Standards. Griffin Press holds
chain of custody certification SGSHK-COC-005088. FSC®
promotes environmentally responsible, socially beneficial
and economically viable management of the world's forests.

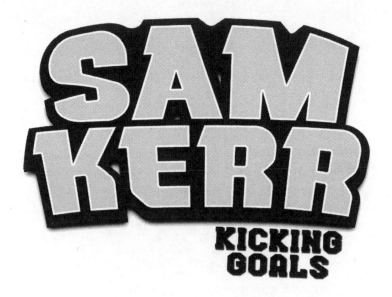

SAM KERR
KICKING GOALS

Sam Kerr and Fiona Harris
Illustrated by Aki Fukuoka

SPORTS DAY

SIMON &
SCHUSTER

London · New York · Sydney · Toronto · New Delhi

CHAPTER ONE

EAST FREMANTLE PRIMARY SCHOOL
MONDAY
9.05 am

'Did you go to the MCG?'

'Yeah!' Dylan says. 'We saw the Carlton–Melbourne game.'

'No way!' I squeal.

I stare at my best friend in amazement. I'm so jealous I can hardly *breathe*! I mean, it's only one of my biggest dreams in the

WORLD to go to Melbourne one day and watch a game at the *actual* Melbourne Cricket Ground, the place where AFL football began!

Dylan grins. 'Yeah, it was awesome.'

It's day one of term two and the whole school has gathered in the hall for our first assembly. Three hundred students are all sitting cross-legged on the cold hardwood floor waiting for it to begin, and the noise echoes around the hall and bounces off the walls. It sounds like Subiaco Oval on game day in here! The preps are definitely the loudest. I can hear them all the way from the back of the hall where us Grade Sixers always sit.

I'm wedged in between my two best friends, Dylan and Indi, and Dylan has just been telling us about his trip to Melbourne over the Easter holidays.

'Aaaaghhh!' I groan, grabbing my ankles and rocking backwards on the floor. 'I'm SO jealous!'

'*Careful!*'

I glance behind me and see that I've almost fallen straight into Chelsea's lap.

'Sorry,' I giggle.

A couple of months ago I would never have dared giggle at the school's bully, Chelsea Flint. But I'm not as scared of her as I used to be now that we're on the same soccer team. Chelsea glares at me for a moment, then goes back

to whispering with her best friend, Nikita.

'I brought you a record from the game,' Dylan tells me. 'I'll give it to you at recess.'

'Thanks,' I say. 'I guess it's the next best thing to being there … kind of.'

Indi whacks me on the leg. 'What are you whinging about?' she cries. 'You caught the biggest fish anyone at the caravan park has seen in twenty years!'

The Pappas family has a caravan at the Myalup Beach Caravan Park and this time I tagged along on their Easter break. Indi's dad and two of her brothers, George and Ari, took me fishing and I caught a whopping big Samson fish, which was super exciting. Indi hates fishing so she stayed back with her mum and her big sister, Rena, at the caravan and read her Harry Potter book instead.

I beam. 'Yeah, I did.'

'My dad spent the whole holiday teasing George and Ari because Sam's fish was bigger than theirs,' Indi tells Dylan. 'They were gutted.' She pauses and grins. 'Get it? Gutted?'

Dylan and I roll our eyes. 'Yeah, we get it,' I say.

'I know you didn't see a game at the MTG, but we still had a great holiday, didn't we?' Indi says, pretending to be hurt.

'It's the MCG, not MTG,' I say, laughing, 'and yes, I had the BEST holiday with you!'

I had the best time back at home, too. Dad surprised me by taking me to watch my first professional soccer game in Perth. It was amazing! They were SO fast, and their passing was sensational! I spent a lot of time watching the players' feet and picked up a few tips and tricks to use myself when I'm back playing with my team, the Knights.

I sigh as I watch our Principal, Mrs Godfrey, walk to the microphone at the front of the hall and hold up her hand, the signal for us all to stop talking so she can start the boring assembly.

'Good morning, everyone,' Mrs Godfrey says. 'I hope you all had a lovely break and are looking forward to an exciting term two!'

As Mrs Godfrey starts talking about dates for maths competitions and renovations on the school playground, my mind wanders and I start to wriggle around on the hard, cold floor. After two weeks of being free to run around and kick a ball as much as I wanted, it's not easy having to sit still for so long.

I look over to the side of the hall where all the teachers are standing along the windows and see Mr Morton frowning at me. I instantly stop my wriggling.

Indi suddenly gasps beside me and I turn to look at her. 'What?'

'Did you hear what Mrs Godfrey just said?' Indi whispers, her eyes wide.

'No, what?'

'Auditions for the school play are next week!' Indi says in a high-pitched whispery voice. '*Peter Pan!*'

'You have to audition!' I whisper.

'I know! I'd LOVE to play the role of Peter Pan!' Indi says, her high-pitched whispery voice getting louder by the second.

A girl in our class, Yvie, turns around and frowns at us. 'SSSSHHHHH!'

I turn back to Mrs Godfrey and notice that she's saying something involving the word 'sport'.

'What's she saying?' I whisper to Dylan.

He turns to me and frowns. 'Listen and you'll hear!'

'. . . and I know Sports Day is one of the biggest events in the school year,'

Mrs Godfrey continues, 'so I'm sure you'll all want to sign up for your favourite activity on the day.'

Sports Day! Awesome!

'I'm going to invite our new sports teacher, Miss McLeish, to come up here now to talk some more about it,' Mrs Godfrey says.

She hands the microphone to someone behind her and every student in the hall cranes their neck to check out our school's new sports teacher. We all loved Mr Scott, but he and his wife moved to Sydney at the end of last term so we've been wondering who his replacement will be.

A small, fit-looking woman in leggings and a red T-shirt steps forward. She has a high black ponytail, sunglasses on top of her head and a big smile on her face.

'Hello students,' she says. 'I'm looking forward to getting to know you all in sports class, but right now I'm going to read through the list of events for Sports Day.'

Dylan and I exchange excited looks.

'On offer this year is netball, athletics, football, cricket and volleyball,' Miss McLeish says. 'Quite a few options there, so I'm sure each of you will find something you enjoy.'

There's no mention of soccer and I feel disappointed, even though I know I shouldn't be surprised. Soccer has never been part of our school's Sports Day.

Up until a couple of months ago I wouldn't have cared at all, but now I can't imagine a Sports Day without it. I slump over and start picking at my shoelaces. With no soccer on the agenda, Sports Day will be okay, but not as good as it could be.

Suddenly, a thought pops into my brain and I sit bolt upright. *Why shouldn't soccer be on the list?* It's a sport too — a REALLY awesome sport that millions of people all over the world play. So, why can't we play it at our school, too? Maybe it's time to shake things up on Sports Day this year!

I'm going to talk to Miss McLeish and convince her to put soccer on her list. The big question now is: how exactly do I do that?

CHAPTER TWO

MY SCHOOL
TUESDAY
10.30 am

After assembly yesterday I spent the rest of
the day zoning out as Mr Morton droned
on about decimals and negative numbers,
trying to think up a good argument for
why Miss McLeish absolutely HAD to
include soccer on the Sports Day line-up.
But by the time I climbed into bed that

night, I was no closer to coming up with a convincing reason for why she should add it to the many other sports that were already in the line-up. Apart from the fact that it's awesome and I REALLY want to play it.

At recess on Tuesday morning, I tell Dylan and Indi my idea to see if they can help.

'Nah, she'll never go for it,' Dylan says, shaking his head at me.

'Why not?' I frown.

'Because no one here cares about soccer, that's why.' Dylan points his muesli bar at me. '*You* didn't care about it until a few months ago.'

'Yeah,' I say, pushing Dylan's nutritious snack away, 'but now I know how good soccer is and I want everyone else to know, too.'

Dylan shrugs. 'Good luck with that.'

'He's right,' Indi adds. 'Footy is the only sport anyone here cares about.'

'Well, thanks for the support, guys,' I say, sarcastically.

'We're just being realistic,' Dylan says. 'No one in Grade Six will want to play soccer on Sports Day.'

I feel like a balloon that's just been pricked with a big fat sharp pin.

'You're probably right,' I sigh. 'I just thought it might be a cool idea, that's all.'

I can see from the looks on their faces that my friends feel bad about bursting my big balloon of joy. They were only being honest with me, like good mates should.

'So, when are the *Peter Pan* auditions?' I ask, nudging Indi with my foot.

'On Friday,' she says, her face lighting up. 'Mr Pinto says I have to learn two scenes if I want to go for Peter.'

'I can help you learn your lines if you want?' I say.

'Cool!' Indi grins. 'Thanks, Sam!'

'I reckon your audition will be *exceptional*, Indi,' Dylan says.

Dylan's dad gave him a book called *Storyteller's Word a Day* last year and every now and then Dylan throws a big fancy word like 'exceptional' into the conversation. It's weird but we're used to it now.

'Hope you're right!' Indi says. 'But it depends on how many other kids are going for the same role.' She laughs. 'I should do a sneaky petition to find out who my competition is!'

My eyes light up, my head whips around and I stare at Indi in delight.

'What?' She frowns. 'Have I got Vegemite on my nose again?'

'A petition!' I cry, jumping up off the grass and slapping my thighs. 'That's it!'

'What's it?' Dylan says, looking confused.

They are both staring at me like I've lost my mind, but I just point over to the bike shed where Miss McLeish is chatting to a bunch of prep girls.

I turn back to my bewildered friends. 'Come with me.'

They shrug and stand up.

'Miss McLeish?' I say, once the giggling gaggle of preps have moved away.

'Hi there!' she says, turning to us with a friendly smile.

'I'm Sam, and this is Dylan and Indi.'

'Nice to meet you all,' Miss McLeish says.

'Um, we just wanted to ask you something about Sports Day.' I feel a tiny bit nervous all of a sudden. 'Um … we were just … uh … wondering if maybe we could have a soccer game on the day, too? It's a really cool sport and we think everyone would love it.'

Miss McLeish frowns and fidgets with the whistle around her neck. 'I don't think that's possible, Sam,' she says gently. 'We already have a lot of sports on the running sheet and I'm not sure we can fit anymore in. Also, there probably wouldn't be enough interest in soccer to justify adding it.'

Ah-ha! I think. *This is where my brilliant idea comes into play!*

'But what if we could find kids who want to play?' I ask, hoping I don't sound as desperate as I feel. 'Like, if they sign a petition?'

Miss McLeish looks thoughtful and my heart leaps.

'Hmmm ... possibly,' she says. 'But I don't know if we have enough time to get it organised and —'

'Please, Miss McLeish!' I definitely sound desperate now, but I don't care anymore. 'Just let us try?'

'If we can garner more interest in it, then it could be a great thing for the school to support a new sport,' Dylan adds.

'Yeah,' I say, assuming that 'garner' is a good thing. 'There might be heaps of kids who've been wanting to play for years!'

'I know I have!' Indi says, stepping forward and placing her hand over her heart. 'I LOVE soccer!'

It takes every bit of willpower in me not to burst out laughing at Indi's performance.

Miss McLeish thinks for a moment, then sighs. 'Okay, I tell you what,' she says.

'If you can get twenty-two signatures on that petition, then we'll do it.'

'Oh, thank you!' I squeal.

'But,' she says, holding a finger up, 'you have to get it to me by Thursday next week or I can't accept it. There's too much planning involved to leave it longer than that. I'll have to amend the Sports Day schedule, organise the umpire and bibs, check with the other teachers ...'

'That's fine!' I say quickly. 'I'll get it to you by then, I promise!'

CHAPTER THREE

THE KNIGHTS' HOME GROUND
TUESDAY
4.15 pm

'Over here, Chelsea!' I shout, running down the pitch at full pelt.

It's later that day and I'm still on a high from getting the go-ahead to start my Sports Day petition, so soccer training is the perfect outlet for all the excited and nervous energy buzzing around inside me.

Chelsea kicks the ball to me and I run down the pitch, nudging it along with my toes for a few seconds before making a quick pass to Toby. As I watch Toby sprint towards our goal, I think about how Chelsea would never have passed to me in a practice match a couple of weeks ago. But she's learnt a bit about playing on a team since then thanks to our coach, Ted, who also happens to be Chelsea's uncle. He says it doesn't matter what's going on between any of us off the pitch. As soon as the game starts, we all need to play as one. Also, she really wants our team to win, just like I do, which is why I've decided to try and get her on board with my Sports Day idea. I just have to pick the right moment.

If I catch Chelsea in a bad mood, I know
I can kiss any chance of her saying yes
goodbye.

'Okay team, over here!' Ted shouts
from the sidelines.

We all jog over, grab our drink bottles
and gather around our coach.

'Great match, guys,' Ted says. 'Now,
at the game on Saturday, I wanna see
you talking to each other just like you
were then.'

Ted tugs on his red Victoria Park cap
and squats down so he's at our eye level.

'As you all know, there are some
important games coming up over the next
few weeks. I reckon we're in with a shot
at the finals at the end of the season if

we keep playing as well as we have been today.'

Dylan and I glance at each other, and I know we're both thinking the same thing. *How cool would it be if we made it to the finals? And in my first year ever playing soccer!*

MY KITCHEN
TUESDAY
6.23 pm

'. . . so then I say to this lady, "I'm sorry but it says on the receipt there are no returns," and then she says, "Oh, I don't read receipts!" '

Maddi stares around the table at all of us, waiting for our shocked reactions.

'I mean, can you believe it?' she cries, stabbing a piece of chicken with her fork. 'Who doesn't read receipts?! All of us in the shop were like, *seriously*?'

While I was catching fish and toasting marshmallows during the Easter holidays, my big sister, Maddi, got herself a part-time job at Shine On, a clothes shop in the mall where Maddi and her friends have been shopping every weekend for the last couple of years. She's spent the last ten minutes telling me, Mum, Dad and Levi one story after another. We've heard about the teenagers who come in with 'truckloads of attitude', the lovely old ladies who tell Maddi she reminds them of their granddaughters, and the excitement she feels when she opens a box of new stock. It's Maddi's dream job. She loves clothes and make up more than life itself, so I guess it would be like me working in a sports shop and being allowed to play with the equipment all day.

'I've never looked at a receipt in my life,' Levi says, grabbing the tomato sauce from the middle of the table and smothering his chicken with it.

'That's cos you've never paid for anything in your life,' Dad says, chuckling.

Mum passes me the brussels sprouts with a nod that says, *Put some of this disgusting green stuff on your plate, please!*

'Daniel called today,' she says. 'He wanted to know how the Knights are going, Sam?'

My oldest brother, Daniel, plays for my AFL team, the West Coast Eagles. The Kerr family have all been obsessed with the Eagles for as long as I can remember, so we were all super excited when Daniel was drafted. We go and cheer him on whenever the Eagles play at Subiaco, which is this weekend!

'What did you tell him?' I ask, trying not to gag as I pick the tiniest brussels sprout I can find out of the bowl.

'I told him you might be in the finals,' Mum says. 'That's right isn't it? Honestly, Sam, could you have found a smaller brussels sprout?'

'Ugh!' Levi scoffs. 'I HATE brussels sprouts.'

'Why do I have to eat them if Levi doesn't?' I say, nodding to Levi's plate, which is completely lacking in anything vaguely resembling a vegetable.

'When you're eighteen you don't have to eat them either,' Mum says. 'But you're still young and need your nutrients.'

'Yeah, Sam,' Levi teases. 'If you want to grow up big and handsome like me you need to eat as many of those slimy little suckers as possible.'

'Ew,' Maddi squeals. '*GAG!*'

'Alright, you lot,' Dad says, waving his fork at us. 'How about we talk about something else. Like the fact that your mother and I will be celebrating our twenty-fifth wedding anniversary in a few weeks.'

'Oh, really?' Maddi says, instantly looking down at her plate. 'Is it that soon?'

There's something weird about the way Maddi says this. I can't put my finger on what it is, but it's a very un-Maddi response. My sister loves her family as much as she loves shopping, so what's with the disinterested tone?

'Wow, I had no idea you've been married that long,' Levi adds.

'Twenty-five years,' Mum says. 'My goodness that has gone so fast.'

'Your mother was the prettiest woman I'd ever seen,' Dad says, smiling at Mum.

'And she fell head over heels in love the minute she laid eyes on me.'

'I think it might have been the other way around actually,' Mum says, her eyes twinkling. 'As I recall, you literally *did* fall. Almost right into my lap. Remember?'

Dad laughs. 'It was all part of my devious plan!'

The four of us Kerr kids have heard this story a million times, but Maddi, Levi and I all smile and laugh in all the right places as Mum and Dad continue to reminisce.

Twenty minutes later, I walk into my bedroom to find our chocolate brown kelpie, Penny, lying on my bed, waiting for me. Just as I'm closing the door behind

me, it flies open again, scaring the life out
of me.

'Hey!' I shout.

Totally ignoring me, Maddi and Levi
come all the way in and shut the door.

'Shush!' Maddi orders.

'Yeah, shush!' Levi hisses.

'What?' I frown. My older brother
and sister NEVER come into my room.
Maddi says it stinks of dirty socks and
dog. To be fair, Penny *does* sleep on my
bed every night, and she *does* enjoy a
good roll in the grass, so she can be
pretty stinky sometimes. I don't mind
though. I'd rather have a stinky Penny
on my bed than no Penny on my bed
at all.

'Why do I have to shush?' I say, folding
my arms and glaring at them.

'Because we don't want Mum and
Dad to know we're in here,' Maddi says,
pushing a pile of soccer magazines off
my green fluffy stool in the corner
and sitting down. Levi plonks himself
down on the floor and leans against
my wardrobe.

'Okay, what's going on?' I ask.

'We're organising a surprise party for
Mum and Dad's wedding anniversary,'
Maddi says.

'Really?' I say, flopping on my bed to
stare at them.

'My idea,' Levi says, puffing his chest
out proudly.

'No, it wasn't,' Maddi snaps. 'It was mine!'

'Anyway, what's the plan?' I say, interrupting before they get stuck in a 'No, you didn't', 'Yes, I did' loop.

'So, their anniversary is on the fourteenth, which is a Friday,' Maddi begins. 'Daniel is going to take them to a fancy afternoon tea somewhere in the city so they're out of the house when we get home from school. Then we'll have a couple of hours to get the house ready for the surprise party.'

'That's why we had to pretend we hadn't remembered when Dad said it at dinner,' Levi says, who is obviously very happy with his acting skills.

'I'm in charge of the invites,' Maddi continues. 'Levi is organising the food. Daniel is getting drinks sorted and you're in charge of picking a theme for the decorations.'

'A theme?' I splutter. 'But I don't know anything about party themes or decorations!'

Levi shrugs. 'So, do some research.'

'We're all pitching in,' Maddi says in her stern 'trying to sound like Mum' voice. 'And you can't give anything away to Mum and Dad, okay? It's a *surprise*.'

'Yeah, I know what surprise means,' I say, rolling my eyes, as Maddi and Levi get up to leave.

As soon as they close the door behind them I turn to Penny. 'An anniversary party theme? I have no clue!'

But Penny just blinks up at me, her tongue hanging out of her mouth, and lays one paw on my leg as if to say, 'Yep. I hear ya, sister.'

CHAPTER FOUR

MY SCHOOL
THURSDAY
9.45 am

'What is it?' Abbie frowns at the piece of paper I've just slid across the table to her.

'It's a petition to let us have a soccer match on Sports Day,' I whisper.

'Soccer?' Abbie screws up her face. 'Who cares about soccer?'

Everything in my body wants to scream, '*I DO!*' but I try to keep my voice friendly. 'It's actually a really cool sport,' I say quietly. 'I reckon everyone would love it if they –'

'*SAM KERR!*'

I look up to see Mr Morton glaring at me over his black-rimmed frames. I quickly cover the petition by sliding my English folder over the top of it.

'Sorry, Mr Morton,' I say.

'Silent reading means being SILENT,' he says. 'Do you think you can manage that?'

I can hear Indi snorting into her sleeve at the table behind me but I don't dare turn around or I'll burst out laughing, too.

Then I'll be in even worse trouble than I
already am.

'Yes, Mr Morton,' I mutter, swallowing
down the giggle burbling around in my
throat.

Mr Morton turns away again, and
I look down at my book. But the words
all blur into one. I can't concentrate. All
I can think about is how to convince Abbie
and everyone else in Grade Six to sign my
'Starting a Soccer Team for Sports Day'
petition.

Once I'm sure that Mr Morton is
distracted with his work again, I slowly
and quietly slide the sheet across to
Josh who is sitting on the other side of
the table.

'Hey, can you sign this?' I whisper.

Without even checking to see what it is, Josh picks up his pen and signs his name under Dylan's.

I don't believe it. How easy was that!

'Thanks!' I mouth as he slides it back.

'What is it?' he whispers.

I hold the sheet up and point to the title at the top. Josh's brow instantly furrows.

'I hadn't planned on playing anything ... but I guess ... maybe ...'

'Thanks, Josh!' I say, quickly slipping the sheet inside my folder before he grabs it back to rub his name out. Anyway, once he starts training and realises how cool soccer is, he'll thank me.

As soon as the bell goes for recess,
I head straight for Chelsea's table. Chelsea
is usually a bit calmer after silent reading
so this morning I decided that today was
the day to ask her to sign.

I place the sheet down in front of her.
'Hey, can you sign this please? I'm trying
to get Miss McLeish to include a soccer
match as part of Sports Day.'

Chelsea glances at the sheet then back
up at me with a sickly sweet smile on her
face. My heart sinks. I know what that fake
smile means.

'Nup,' she chirps. 'I'm not signing
that.'

Nikita leans over to take a look. 'What
is it?' she asks.

'It's a petition,' I say, trying not to sound as desperate as I feel. 'I need a bunch of signatures to take to Miss McLeish.'

I turn back to Chelsea. 'I thought you'd want to play soccer on Sports Day since you, ya know, play it and all.'

Chelsea shrugs. 'I don't want to sign it,' she says, standing up. 'Come on, Nik.'

The two of them walk out and I stare after them in total disbelief. Indi appears behind me and slings her arm around my shoulders.

'What is wrong with her?' I say, turning to Indi. 'Why won't she sign it?'

'She doesn't want you taking the glory for creating the first school soccer team,'

Indi says matter-of-factly. 'You know what Chelsea's like.'

'But she PLAYS soccer! I thought she'd want to show off her skills in front of the whole school!'

'Nah,' Indi says, shaking her head. 'She'd hate for you to show her up in front of everyone.'

'Yep,' Dylan says, popping up next to Indi and shaking his head. 'That's Chelsea. The *consummate* attention-seeker.'

I have no idea what 'consummate' means, but I know my friends are right. I probably have zero chance of getting Chelsea to sign my petition.

'What are we going to do?' I moan to my friends. 'We only have five signatures, including mine and Dylan's, and we have to get this petition to Miss McLeish in a week. That's not enough time!'

CHAPTER FIVE

MY SCHOOL
FRIDAY
4.15 pm

The following afternoon I'm still wracking my brain to think of a way to get more signatures while I wait for Indi to come out of her *Peter Pan* audition. I wanted to be there to give her moral support in case it all went badly, which I'm 99.999 per cent sure it won't.

Sitting alone in the quiet schoolyard is actually the perfect time to think about my petition problem.

Maybe I could offer a free chocolate bar with every signature?

Nah ... there's no way my pocket money would cover that.

What if I organised for the whole Perth soccer team to come and do a demo at the school to prove how awesome it is?

Nah, probably not. I don't have any of the players' phone numbers.

'*SAM*!'

Indi runs down the steps, glowing with happiness. A dozen or so other kids trail behind her.

I stand up and grin. 'So, from the look on your face, I'm guessing you totally nailed it in there?'

'Ssshhh!' Indi says, pulling me away from the rest of the kids. 'I don't know yet. They didn't tell us who got what parts, but ...'

'But?'

She looks around to make sure no one can hear. 'But yeah, I totally nailed it!'

'YES!' I shout.

We high-five and I launch into two backflips on the grass, one after another, before running back to throw my arms around her shoulders.

Indi laughs. 'Man, I hope I get it.'

'Of course you will,' I say. I've watched Indi act heaps of times and she's a natural. How could she *not* get the role?

'It was SO much fun!' she says as we walk out of the school gate and onto the street. 'Are you sure you don't want to audition, too? Maybe for a Lost Boy or a pirate? I could totally see you sword-fighting your way across the stage!'

'Nah, I'm good thanks,' I say.

'Maybe I can talk Dylan into auditioning,' Indi says. 'Miss Mitchell said they need more boys in the show.'

'No way! He'd be even more freaked out than me!'

'Probably,' Indi says. 'Hey, do you reckon he got any more signatures on the petition?'

'I hope so ...'

As I went off to wait for Indi, Dylan said he'd stand at the school gate and try to get

some more signatures as kids headed home.
I'm worried he might not have been pushy
enough. Or that he would have used his
big words that no one understands. That
would definitely put people off.

'Come on,' Indi says, pulling me along
the street. 'He'll be at my place soon so we
can find out how many he got.'

CHAPTER SIX

INDI'S HOUSE

FRIDAY

4.40 pm

'Three?' I groan. 'Only three more signatures?' I slump onto the floor. That makes it just eight in total, which is nowhere near the twenty-two we need.

Indi throws her bag next to the couch then sits cross-legged next to me, her knee touching mine.

'I tried to get more,' Dylan says, still standing in the doorway to Indi's lounge room, 'but as soon as I said the word "soccer" everyone screwed up their faces like I'd just offered them a poo sandwich.'

Dylan grabs a handful of Cheezels out of the bowl on the coffee table and collapses into the velvet bean bag in the corner.

'Why is everyone hating on soccer?' I say, throwing my hands up.

Dylan raises one eyebrow. 'Don't you remember how you *recoiled* when I first asked *you* to play soccer at the start of this year?' he says, shoving three whole Cheezels in his mouth.

'Yeah, okay,' I mutter. Dylan's right. I'd never given soccer a second thought

until earlier this year. I'd been playing
footy since I was seven and was an AFL girl
through and through.

Suddenly Indi sighs loudly enough to put
out a small fire and falls backwards onto
the grey fluffy rug, arms splayed out at her
sides, in typical dramatic Indi style.

'Okay, I'll sign up,' she says.

Dylan and I stare at her.

'You?' I say.

'Yeah, why not,' she says, sitting up.

'But … you … don't … know …
anything … about … soccer.' I speak
really slowly, the way I do when I want
Penny to understand what I'm saying.

'Neither did you a few months ago,'
Indi says.

'But you ... I mean, you're not ...'
Dylan says, looking as shocked as I feel.

'Sporty?' Indi says. 'I know, but last
term you both came to my acting class,
right? Even though I know you HATE
getting up in front of people. So, why can't
I play sport for you now? That's how it's
supposed to work with friends, right?'

Part of me is totally grateful to my
best friend for wanting to help us out
like this, but a bigger part knows that
Indi can barely catch or throw a ball, let
alone kick one along the grass in a
straight line.

'Well, I don't know if ...'

Indi explodes. 'I thought you needed
names! I'm trying to help you out!'

'I've got it!' Dylan slaps the bean bag making us both jump. 'What if Indi was a goalie?'

'Uh …'

'What does a goalie do?' Indi asks.

'Stands in front of the net and tries to stop balls going into it,' Dylan says.

Indi nods firmly as if it's a done deal. 'Cool, I can do that,' she says.

I'm still not 100 per cent convinced that this is a good idea, but I'm also not in any position to say no to someone who wants to sign our petition.

'Okay,' I say. 'Deal!'

'Hey, gang!'

Indi's mum, Mrs Pappas, enters the loungeroom wearing denim overalls

and holding some kind of dirt-covered gardening tool in her hand.

'Hi Mrs Pappas,' Dylan and I chime in unison.

'Hey Mum, guess what?' Indi says proudly. 'I'm gonna be a goalie on the school soccer team.'

Mrs Pappas bursts out laughing, then stops when she notices her daughter's hurt expression.

'Oh, sorry darling,' she says, leaning down to stroke Indi's auburn curls. 'I thought you were joking. I'm sure you'll be *fovero*!'

Indi rolls her eyes, but I can tell she's not as upset as she's pretending to be.

'Shall I order the pizza now?' Mrs Pappas asks. 'Same as usual?'

We all nod vigorously. 'Yes, please!'

Every third Friday night, Dylan, Indi and I have a pizza and movie night at one of our houses and our orders never change. It's a Capricciosa for Dylan, Margherita with salami for Indi, and Pepperoni for me.

'Hey!' Dylan slaps the bean bag again, making us jump for the second time in two minutes.

'Will you stop doing that?' I say.

'Sorry,' Dylan says, then turns to Indi. 'How did the audition go?'

'She was *fantastikós*!' Mrs Pappas cries.

'Mum!' Indi squeals. 'You weren't even there! And I was not fantastic.'

'Of course you were!' Mrs Pappas grabs one of Indi's cheeks with her spare hand and squeezes it. 'My little Nicole Kidman!'

Dylan and I rock with laughter as Indi squirms out of her mum's grasp.

'You do kind of resemble Nicole Kidman,' Dylan says. 'You have the same curly hair.'

Indi rolls her eyes. 'Yeah, if Nicole Kidman was Greek and wore glasses,' she says, but I can tell she's flattered by the comparison.

'Nicole Kidman wishes she was Greek,' Indi's brother George says as he enters the room and grabs a handful of Cheezels.

'George!' says Mrs Pappas. 'Those aren't for you!'

'Sorry,' he says, grinning at me as he shoves a whole handful in his mouth.

'Come on,' Mrs Pappas says, pushing George towards the door. 'I need you to come and help me move some of the outdoor pots before Dad gets home.'

'He won't be happy,' George says, shaking his head.

The two of them walk out and I smile at the thought of Mr Pappas coming home and finding that his wife has moved all his pot plants around. Uh-oh. That reminds me. I haven't even thought about the theme for my mum and dad's party yet.

'I need your help,' I say, turning back to my friends.

'We know, Sam!' Indi says. 'We're trying to think of a way to get more signatures!'

I shake my head. 'No, I have ANOTHER problem.'

'Oh, geez,' Dylan drops his head in his hands. 'What now?'

'Do either of you have any theme ideas for my mum and dad's surprise anniversary party?' I ask. 'Maddi and Levi put me in charge, and I have no idea where to –'

'Oh my god,' Indi squeals, leaping to her feet and clapping her hands together. 'I have LOADS of ideas! Wait, just let me grab my design scrapbook!'

She runs out of the room and Dylan and I turn to stare at each other in amazement.

'Did she just say "scrapbook"?'

'Um, yeah. She did,' Dylan says, looking just as confused as me.

'Wow,' I say. 'Our best friend is a scrapbooker. Who knew?'

CHAPTER SEVEN

THE KNIGHTS' HOME GROUND
SATURDAY
3.15 pm

'Ky, just remember to be aware of where your teammates are. You had a great opportunity to get the ball to Jai near goal at one point,' Ted says. 'Dylan, great work anticipating where the ball was going. And fantastic passing, Archie and Sam. Chelsea, excellent defence!'

It's half-time in our game against the Avengers, and the score is 1–2 their way. Noah has scored our only goal so far, and we just have to hope we can get more goals in the next half.

My whole family is here today – Mum, Dad, Maddi, Levi and Daniel – but at least half of them come every week. As I'm walking back onto the pitch, Levi waves his sausage sandwich at me and a big glob of tomato sauce drips onto his hoodie. Mum immediately opens her handbag to get a tissue and Maddi rolls her eyes. Daniel gives me a thumbs up and Dad cups his hands around his mouth and shouts, *'GO KNIGHTS!'*

The second half starts out pretty well. We're all pumped after Ted's half-time

pep talk and go out onto the pitch full of determination. When Dylan scores a goal in the first five minutes, the Knights spectators go crazy. It's such a great goal and totally unexpected. Dylan, Chelsea and Archie did some sensational quick-fire passing down the pitch until Dylan eventually booted it straight into the corner of the net, just managing to dodge an Avengers player at the last second. It's so exciting that I do a backflip right there in the middle of the pitch.

But sadly, that's my last backflip for the whole match. In the final few minutes, one of the Avengers heads the ball straight into the back of their goal net and it's game over. The whistle blows and we've lost.

We smile and shake hands with the other team, but all of us feel flat and miserable as we trudge slowly off the pitch.

Ted greets us with a big smile. 'Well done, team,' he says as we sink onto the grass in a circle around him. 'You played a great game and they just got the better of us in the end. But don't worry. We still have another chance at making the finals. It's not over yet!'

Ted's optimism makes me feel a bit better, but only a tiny bit. I start running through the game in my head and thinking about all the things I could have done differently. *If only I'd swerved left instead of right that Avengers player wouldn't have been able to intercept it like he did. And maybe*

I should have just shot for goal that time I was running towards it instead of passing to Chelsea. Then again, I know there was no way I could have made that shot. I had to pass.

These thoughts bounce around my brain as I suck on my water bottle and listen to my teammates mumbling about how we should have won that game. Finally, I have to admit to myself that thinking this way isn't doing any good. The game is over, and we lost. Simple as that.

And Ted's right. We still have another chance so it's not the end of the world.

CHAPTER EIGHT

MY ROOM
SUNDAY
10.15 am

'These ideas are awesome!' Maddi
says. 'And you came up with all these
yourself?'

For a moment I think about lying to
Maddi and Levi so they'll think I'm some
kind of creative genius, but then decide to
come clean.

'No, Indi helped me,' I confess. 'Like, a lot.'

'I love it!' Maddi cries, flipping through a bunch of different party decoration images I've printed out. 'Mum will love the balloon arch and photo wall, and Dad will flip his lid over the footy-shaped lights. Good work, Sammy!'

'Thanks,' I say, my face flushing at hearing my big sister praise me.

Maddi, Levi and I have secretly gathered in Maddi's VERY neat bedroom so we can talk about the party without Mum and Dad hearing us. It smells nice in here. No stinky soccer socks or mud-caked soccer balls in the corner, only fairy lights, Destiny's Child posters and the smell of some kind of flowery perfume.

Maddi turns her attention to our brother who is rolling around on her Moroccan rug with Penny.

'What have you organised, Levi?' she asks. 'LEVI?'

'Huh?' Levi peeks out from under Penny's giant brown head. 'Oh, um ... I spoke to Dave at the deli down the road and he's gonna do up some antipasto platters and quiches and stuff.'

Maddi nods approvingly. 'Okay, good. Did you ask about vegetarian options?'

Levi frowns. 'No!'

Maddi rolls her eyes. 'Well make sure you do,' she says, pointing one perfectly manicured pink fingernail at him.

Levi gently pushes Penny off him, sits up and salutes our sister. 'Yes, Boss!' he barks.

'Maddi?'

Our heads whip around in panic at the sound of Mum's voice close outside the bedroom door.

Maddi nods at the printed pages at my feet. 'Quick, put them under the bed!'

I manage to get them out of sight just as Mum opens Maddi's door.

'Have you seen my ...?'

She stops when she sees the three of us (four including Penny) sitting on Maddi's floor, with giant, guilty smiles frozen onto our faces.

Mum frowns. 'What are you three doing?'

'Nothing,' we all say in unison.

Mum raises one eyebrow. 'Since when do you all hang out in Maddi's room?' She nods at Levi and me. 'I didn't think either of you was even allowed in here.'

'We're ... um ... we're ...' Maddi stammers.

'... teaching Maddi the rules of soccer!'

Three human heads, and one canine head, turn to look at me.

'Really?' Mum says. Both eyebrows are way up near her hairline now.

'Yep,' Maddi says, nodding like a maniac. 'I ... um ... asked Sam to teach me the rules so I can ... um ... know what to shout out when I go to her game on the weekend.'

'Riiiiight … and what was that you shoved under the bed then?' Mum asks.

'Game plans!' Levi adds.

Mum clearly doesn't believe a word of any of this. But she just looks at each of us in turn and sighs. 'Okay, I'll let you get back to it,' she says. 'I just wanted to know if you've seen the good pen and notepad I keep next to the phone?'

We all know that the objects in question are behind Maddi's back, covered in party plans, but we just shake our heads.

'Nope, haven't seen them,' Maddi says.

'Okaaaaay,' she says slowly. 'Just make sure you're all ready to leave for the footy in an hour, okay?'

'Yep!' I say.

The West Coast Eagles are playing
Hawthorn at Subiaco today so the whole
Kerr family is heading off to watch the
game. Mum shoots us one final quizzical
look and backs out of the room.

As soon as the door shuts behind her,
we all let out a collective sigh of relief.

Maddi throws her hands in the air.
'Teaching me about soccer?' she whispers.
'Really, Sam? That's the best you could
come up with?'

'At least I came up with something!'
I shoot back. 'You two didn't say a word!'

Levi shrugs. 'I thought it was genius.'

'Sorry, but I've got soccer on the brain,'
I say.

'What's new?' Maddi sighs.

I shake my head. 'No, I mean more than usual.'

'Why?' Levi asks. 'What's up?'

I tell them both about the deal I have with Miss McLeish, the soccer petition and my classmates' total lack of interest in signing it. When I finish talking, Maddi shrugs as if it's a no-brainer.

'You just have to approach it with a sales brain,' she says.

'What does that mean?' I ask.

'You've gotta SELL soccer to them,' Maddi explains. 'Make them *want* to buy it. Like when we want to sell a certain dress or top in the shop, we put it in the window and put pretty flowers and cool scarves and stuff around it, so it gets customers' attention.'

'But how do I do that?' I ask. 'I can't really put pretty flowers around a petition.'

'Have you heard of David Beckham?' Maddi says.

'Der!' I cry. 'Of *course* I have! He's only the best soccer player in the world!'

'He's also the cutest!' Maddi says. 'If you add a photo of cute Beckham in action to your sign-up sheet, then everyone will want to sign it because they'll either be in love with him, or they'll want to BE him.'

'She's right,' Levi says, flopping backwards to wrestle with Penny again. 'People love an action pic.'

'That's an awesome idea!' I squeal. 'Thanks!'

'Levi! You're vacuuming all that dog hair out of my rug,' Maddi says as she watches Penny rolling around and shedding bucketloads of hair. 'Gross!'

I jump up and head for the door.

'Where are you going?' Maddi says.

'To the print shop before they close! I'm gonna print out a full A4 glossy action shot of Beckham and take it to school on Monday!'

I grab my wallet out of my room, tell Mum I'll be back in time to go to the footy and feel full of a new hope as I leave the house.

This soccer team might just happen after all!

CHAPTER NINE

MY SCHOOL
MONDAY
10.55 am

'I'm Peter Pan!'

Indi looks like she's about to burst with excitement.

'YAY!' I throw my arms around her and the two of us jump up and down in the middle of the school oval.

'You're going to be a *magnificent* Peter!'

Dylan says, high-fiving her. 'I can just see you flying across the stage, totally rocking those green tights!'

'Thanks guys,' Indi says, blushing. 'And guess what? That's not the only good news today ...'

'What?' I ask. 'Did you win an Oscar or something as well?'

'Follow me,' she says with a sly grin.

Two minutes later, Dylan and I are standing in front of the noticeboard in the school corridor, staring up at my petition in amazement.

'It's almost full!' I cry.

'I know!' Indi squeals. 'I ran to check it as soon as I came out of the hall. Can you believe it? Maddi's idea worked.'

It sure did. Underneath the super glossy action shot of David Beckham playing in the 2002 World Cup there are now nine more signatures.

'WOAH!' Dylan says. 'That's sensational! And we still have till Thursday to get the last five signatures we need!'

Now I'm the one feeling so happy I could burst, until I scan the names on the sheet and realise that one person is still missing.

CHAPTER TEN

THE KNIGHTS' HOME GROUND
TUESDAY
4.40 pm

'Why won't you sign the petition?'
I narrow my eyes at Chelsea as we kick
the ball back and forth to each other.
Ted has paired us up for passing drills at
training today and for the first time ever,
I wasn't upset at being stuck with her.
She can't just walk away this time, and

with Nikita not around, there's more of a chance she'll talk to me. I'm going to find out once and for all why she won't sign the petition.

'I've got it in my bag if you want to sign it now,' I say. 'I thought you, more than anyone, would want Sports Day to include soccer.'

'Nope,' Chelsea shrugs, dribbling the ball around the cones and then kicking it across the dewy grass to me. 'I'm thinking about signing up for netball.'

I stop the ball under my foot and stare at her. 'Netball? Okay, but can't you do both? I thought you'd want to play soccer, too. You're a great player and we need people like you to fill out the teams.'

I pass her the ball and she traps it under her right foot, holding it there for a moment. I watch her face closely and I can tell she's thinking about it.

Suddenly Chelsea lets out a huge sigh. 'Fine!' she says, rolling her eyes and starting to dribble the ball around her cones. 'I'll sign your stupid sheet. But I'm only doing it because I don't want soccer getting a bad rep if you fill the teams with bad players.'

'Great, thanks,' I say, trying not to look too excited in case she takes it back. 'I'll give it to you after training.'

'Whatever,' Chelsea shrugs.

She kicks the ball back to me with such force that it whizzes past me and hits Cooper square in the back of the head.

'Hey!' he shouts from behind me where he's doing the same drill with Dylan.

'Sorry,' Chelsea smiles sweetly.

CHAPTER ELEVEN

JOE'S PIZZA PLACE
TUESDAY
5.30 pm

'To the Knights!' Ted cries, raising his lemonade.

'*THE KNIGHTS!*' we all echo, raising our soft drinks and clinking them against each other's. It feels like every single person in the restaurant turns to glare at us for being too noisy, but

we're all having too much fun to
care.

Ted has brought us out to Joe's Pizza
Place, straight from training at the Bruce
Lee Oval. I never get a chance to talk to
my teammates at trainings or games, other
than to shout at them to pass me the ball or
to yell 'Great goal!', but tonight I've learnt
heaps more about them.

Archie is a gun swimmer and has to get
up at five am three mornings a week to
train before going to school. Ugh! I can't
think of anything WORSE than having
to get up that early! I also found out that
Jai's dad used to play AFL at the same club
where my dad played, and that James has
three dogs, all Labradors.

Dylan is sitting across from me and we ended up sharing a large Margherita with pepperoni. It was so delicious that we finished the whole thing, but now I'm so full that I can't imagine ever being hungry again.

'Who wants ice-cream?' Ted asks.

On second thoughts, I could probably squeeze a teeny tiny bit more in …

'Me please!' I shout, along with everyone else.

Ten minutes later, I'm scooping the last bit of chocolate ice-creamy goodness from my bowl when Ted leans over and taps Dylan on the arm.

'How's the ankle feeling, Dylan?' he asks.

Dylan sprained his ankle last term during a game, and we were all worried he wouldn't be able to play for ages. But it healed really well and now he's back in action.

All heads turn to look at Dylan.

'Splendid, thanks,' he says softly.

Ted's eyebrows shoot up. '*Splendid*!' he repeats. 'Good word!'

'Yeah, he does that,' I say proudly. 'Comes out with good words.'

Dylan's neck starts doing its blotchy, red thing and I wonder if I shouldn't have drawn more attention to him when I can tell he's already embarrassed with everyone looking.

'Yeah, my ankle is fine, Ted,' Dylan says, looking down into his bowl of choc-chip ice-cream.

'I thought it must be,' Ted grins. 'You're playing really well out there. Thank goodness it healed so quickly.'

'And we've got Sports Day at school coming up, too,' Dylan says. 'I would have hated missing out on that.'

Ted leans forward with interest. He loves talking about sport. *Any* sport.

'Oh yeah?' he says. 'When's that?'

'Not for a few weeks,' Dylan says, then nods at me. 'Sam is trying to get the school to let us have a soccer match on the day, too. They've never included soccer on Sports Day before so it's a pretty big deal.'

'That's fantastic!' Ted says, turning to look at me. 'Good work, Sam. We need more people getting the word out about how awesome soccer is.'

'Thanks,' I say, feeling my own face flushing red as everyone turns to look at me. 'We don't have enough signatures yet, though, so it might not happen.'

Ted frowns, confused. 'What do you mean?'

I explain the deal I have with Miss McLeish. 'We got a couple more signatures today,' I say, glancing at Chelsea down the other end of the table, 'but we still need three more, and if we don't get them by Thursday, it's all over. No soccer game.'

'Well, that would be a shame,' Ted says, looking genuinely disappointed for us. 'I hope you get them in time.'

He turns to look at Chelsea. 'You didn't tell me about this, Chels,' he says, then grins at the rest of us. 'Probably worried her uncle will come down to the school and embarrass her on the sidelines. Chelsea would have been the first person to sign that sheet, I'm guessing?'

Chelsea blushes. 'Um … well …'

'She was!' I say, glancing at Chelsea.

'I'm not surprised,' Ted beams. 'I'm proud of you three for getting the word out about our fantastic sport. I'm sure you'll have no trouble getting the last few signatures and I'll definitely come down to cheer you all on!'

I sneak a look at Chelsea at the other end of the table, and she is as red as the little squares on the tablecloth under her hands. As I'm looking, she glances up and gives me the teensiest tiniest smile of gratitude in the world.

I'll take it!

CHAPTER TWELVE

MY SCHOOL
THURSDAY
1.10 pm

'Okay, you go to the log playground and ask Lenny and his mates,' I tell Dylan, 'and Indi and I will go to the green steps and ask Finn and her group. Meet back here in ten, got it?'

'Copy that!' Dylan says, then races off towards the playground, as Indi and I bolt in the opposite direction.

It's the start of lunchtime on Thursday and we have just twenty minutes to get the fully signed petition to Miss McLeish or our soccer dream will be over. We've got twenty-one signatures now, so need just one more to seal the deal. You wouldn't think it would be so hard to get one measly signature, but it feels like the universe is against us today.

We had ZERO chance of getting our last signature in class this morning. Mr Morton was on the warpath – he was grumpier than I've ever seen him before, and I've seen him REALLY grumpy. He made us do fraction worksheets in 'COMPLETE AND TOTAL SILENCE' and looked straight at me when he said it. How rude!

At recess all of Grade Six had to go straight to the hall to practise our school song for assembly. Then we had assembly and Mr Morton would have seen it for sure if I'd tried to smuggle the form in. With the mood he's in today, I don't even want to think about what he would have done if he'd caught me.

So now the three of us are in a frantic panic to get that last signature.

I thrust the sheet in front of Finn and from the look on her face I know straight away that our luck isn't about to change.

'Yeah-nah, I don't know anything about soccer,' Finn says.

'You could learn!' I say, desperately. 'I've seen you playing down ball and you've got awesome hand–eye coordination skills.'

Finn frowns. 'But you're not allowed to use your hands in soccer, are you?'

She's got a point there. 'Well, no, but ...'

'... you have to have quick feet!' Indi quickly jumps in to save me. 'And you *definitely* have that in down ball.'

For a moment I think Finn might be about to say yes, then she shakes her head and my heart sinks. 'Nah, sorry Sam.'

I turn to the girls next to her, Abbie, Chloe and Manaal, but I can see that it's a lost cause. All three of them are already shaking their heads.

'Okay,' I say glumly. 'No worries.'

'We still have eighteen minutes,' Indi says, looking at her watch as we walk away. 'Don't panic yet.'

'Maybe Dylan had more luck,' I say hopefully. 'Come on, let's go back.'

But Dylan's expression tells us everything we need to know.

'Lenny and his mates have already signed up for footy and aren't interested in playing soccer as well,' Dylan says glumly.

'Come on,' I say. 'Let's start at the bike sheds and go from one end of the yard to the other. There has to be at least ONE kid we haven't thought of yet!'

But thirteen minutes later our hopes are quickly fading. We've asked every kid we could find and not one of them, apart from the ones who've already signed up, is interested. I feel like crying.

'The bell is going in five minutes,' I say, flopping down onto the steps of the art room. 'It's over.'

Dylan nods sadly in agreement, but Indi frowns at us.

'I can't believe you're both giving up so easily,' she scolds. 'Where's that fighting spirit you sporty guys are meant to have?'

'Indi,' I say, 'we have literally asked every single kid and …'

But I stop when I see someone in the distance. Indi and Dylan follow my stare and all three of us gasp in unison.

'Lily Hallington!'

'Let's go!' I say, jumping up to run in the direction of our last hope.

Lily Hallington is a sports NUT! Even more so than me, and I know for a fact that her dad is English, and that Lily has played every sport from indoor cricket to football. I can't believe I didn't think of her earlier! But Lily is one of those kids who is super quiet and keeps to herself. I've been at school with Lily for almost seven years but don't think I've ever had a conversation with her. I just have to hope that our first-ever chat goes the way I want!

'Lily!'

She turns around with a start and stares at the three of us wide-eyed. We must look a bit crazy, standing there with manic grins frozen on our faces.

'Um ... hi?' she says nervously.

'How's it going?' Indi starts. 'We were wondering if ...'

'We need your help!' I blurt out.

Lily frowns. 'With what?'

I give her the lightning-speed version of our situation, finishing with, 'and we need to get it on Miss McLeish's desk in two minutes or there will be no more chances! Can you please, *please* help us?!'

Lily stares at me for a second and then her mouth begins to twitch. 'You're pretty desperate huh?'

'YES!' the three of us cry in unison.

It seems like an hour passes as Lily stares at us, although it's probably only five seconds, then she shrugs and grabs the pen out of my hand.

'Sure,' she says, leaning over to sign the sheet. 'Why not? Dad's been wanting me to play soccer for ages. Besides, I'm worried you're going to pass out if you don't start breathing again pretty soon, Sam!'

I realise then that I've been holding my breath since the moment I finished my desperate rant.

I let out my breath in a big woosh and reach over to grab a startled Lily in a giant bear hug.

'Thank you! Thank you so much!' I yell. 'I can't tell you how much we —'

'Sam!' Dylan barks. 'You can thank her later!' He points at Indi's watch. 'You've gotta go, now!'

I look at the watch and my heart starts to beat like crazy.

It's 1.29!

The bell is going to ring at any second!

CHAPTER THIRTEEN

MY SCHOOL
THURSDAY
1.29 pm

'GO!' Indi shouts.

I turn and bolt towards Miss McLeish's office as fast as my legs will carry me. I don't think I've ever run so fast in my whole life! Ted would be proud.

Chelsea and Nikita are sitting right in the middle of the steps that lead up to the school building, blocking the entrance.

'Get out of the way!' I shout on approach. 'Quick!'

Chelsea's eyes widen in shock but before she can say anything, I take a running leap and vault right over the top of her skinny legs, flying through the air like a possessed kangaroo.

Chelsea squeals as my feet skim the tops of her knees, but I only have time for a quick glance back to make sure I haven't taken out anyone's eye before I continue bolting down the corridor.

I arrive at Miss McLeish's office, waving the form above my head just as the bell goes. A startled Miss McLeish

looks up as I slap the form down on her desk.

'Good grief!' she cries.

'Sorry!' I pant. 'It's just ... we've got the ... it's the form for the ...'

I'm so out of breath I can barely get a sentence out. So, I just point at the form instead, hoping she'll understand.

But when she picks up the form, she doesn't smile or say anything I'm expecting to see or hear.

'We did it,' I say. 'There are enough kids on the sheet for two teams.'

Miss McLeish looks up at me. 'I'm sorry, Sam,' she says, 'but I've already allocated all the areas of the school for the other sports and there's just no way we can fit soccer in at this stage. I didn't think you would get all the people you needed.'

'But you said … we got it in on time and …'

I feel hot tears pricking at the corners of my eyes and blink them away. I don't want to cry in front of a teacher, let alone one who has *lied* to us.

'I know what I said but there's nothing I can do,' she says gently. 'I'm sorry, Sam. Don't you have to get to class now?'

I'm so stunned that I don't even know what to say. I'm not sure I'd be able to speak even if I could find the words. So I just nod, then turn and walk out of her office. It feels like the floor is falling out from under me.

She promised! We got it to her on time!
How can she do this?

These thoughts are still racing round
and round my brain as I enter the
classroom in a daze. I sit down next
to Dylan and Indi whose smiles instantly
vanish when they see the look on
my face.

'Okay, everyone,' Mr Morton says,
putting his glasses on and standing up
from his desk. 'Get your English
workbooks to continue on with your
creative pieces please.'

'What happened?' Indi whispers.

'She said it was too late,' I say, trying
to keep my voice steady and not cry.
'We can't have a soccer team.'

'No way!' Dylan says, his eyes like saucers. 'But she promised!'

'I know, but she said –'

'SAM KERR!' Mr Morton is standing right behind me. 'If it's not bad enough that you arrive late, now you are disrupting the class with your chatter! Take your book and go and work alone at the corner table please.'

I keep my eyes down as I move tables, in case anyone sees the tears welling up in them. But they're not tears of sadness anymore. Now they're angry tears.

The one thing I know for sure as I sit down at the table is that I'm not done with Sports Day just yet. As soon as the school day is finished, I'm going straight back to Miss McLeish to give it one last shot.

After all this work, I'm not giving up this easily.

I arrive at Miss McLeish's office straight after school to find her squatting in the corner and sorting through a bunch of netball bibs.

'Miss McLeish?'

She looks surprised to see me back and a little bit annoyed, too. 'Yes, Sam?'

'I'm sorry, but I just wanted to come back and ask again if there's any chance of us having our soccer team,' I say, trying to keep my voice calm and steady. 'It's just that we put so much work into trying to get those signatures and …'

Miss McLeish sighs and stands up. 'Sam, I told you that it's just not possible,' she says firmly. 'There's nowhere for us to have a soccer match because all the areas are already allocated to other sports. I'm sorry, but there's nothing I can do, so can you please …'

'We could have the soccer match on the grassy area behind the music room,' a deep voice says behind me.

I spin around to see Mr Morton standing in the doorway. He's staring straight at Miss McLeish with a look on his face I know all too well. It's his 'I'm not putting up with this nonsense' look, but for once it's not directed at me.

I turn back to Miss McLeish who seems as shocked as me to see him there. 'Um, well … yes, I suppose that could work.'

'I think it would be worth looking into,' Mr Morton says, still not looking at me. 'The kids have gone to a lot of effort to get those signatures. It would only be right to fulfill the promise made to them don't you think?'

What is happening? Is Mr Morton on our side? Is he trying to help us?

It's like the world has turned upside down. I wouldn't be surprised if trees and bushes start sprouting out from the roof!

Miss McLeish stares back at Mr Morton for a moment before her face suddenly softens.

'You're right, Mr Morton,' she says, nodding. 'I'm sure we can make it work. Okay, Sam. You have your soccer match for Sports Day.'

I feel dizzy with relief and happiness. We did it! And by 'we', I mean Mr Morton, too. Who knew there was a heart beneath that grumpy exterior?

'Thank you, Miss McLeish,' I manage to say. Then I turn to Mr Morton, who is still leaning against the door. 'Thank you, Mr Morton.'

He doesn't say a word, just gives me a short nod and walks away. But I'm

almost 99.5 per cent sure I see a tiny smile

tugging at the corner of his mouth as

he goes.

CHAPTER FOURTEEN

MY ROOM

WEDNESDAY

4.05 pm

'You're next, Hook! This time you've gone too far!' Indi leaps off my bed and brandishes her ruler at an invisible Captain Hook, jumping all over the room, bumping off the wardrobe and the walls.

My bedroom door flies open and Indi spins around to see Maddi standing there, looking confused.

'What the heck is going on in here?'
she says.

'Sorry!' Indi says with a grin. 'Sam's
helping me practise my lines for *Peter Pan*.'

'It's the scene where Peter Pan fights
Captain Hook,' I explain.

'Oohhhh right,' Maddi says, leaning on
the door and grinning. 'I played Tinkerbell
in primary school, you know.'

'Really?' Indi says, looking impressed.
'I didn't know that!'

I clear my throat. 'Um, did you come
in here for a reason, Maddi?' If I don't put
a stop to this now, we'll end up hearing
the whole story about how one of the Lost
Boys forgot his lines and Maddi had to save
the day by whispering them to him.

'Oh, yeah,' Maddi says. 'Mum asked if Indi wants to stay for dinner.' She turns to Indi. 'If it's okay with your mum?'

'Go on!' I say, super excited. It's not often I can have a friend for dinner during the week. 'Call your mum and ask!'

'Okay,' Indi beams. 'I'll ring her now.'

As she runs out to use our phone, Maddi looks over her shoulder then walks a bit further into the room. 'Daniel's picking up all the decorations tomorrow,' she whispers. 'And we've had forty RSVPs so far. It's gonna go off next Friday night!'

She walks out and I suddenly feel a bit nervous at the idea of having so many people here in a week's time for a party that WE have organised. I hope nothing goes wrong at the last minute. We've all been working so hard to keep it a surprise – not an easy thing to do when we all share a house.

Maddi has turned into Party Planner of the Century, which means I can't even walk into the bathroom to brush my teeth without her following me in to ask me if I think the balloon arch should go in the lounge room or the backyard, or if we should get more trestle tables from the footy club, or if we should use Dad's wheelbarrow as a giant esky.

I don't really mind, but it can get pretty annoying when she asks me for the tenth time if I think we have enough chairs.

Especially when the party isn't the only thing taking up my brain space right now.

Ever since Miss McLeish agreed to us having our soccer match on Sports Day three weeks ago, it has been FULL ON!

Miss McLeish made Dylan and me captains of the teams, so we've had so much to do! First off the bat was getting both teams together on the oval at lunchtime to go through the basic rules of soccer. It made me think about my first training session with the Knights and how little I knew about the game. I've learnt heaps since then, but I tried to remember how confusing it was at the start, so I didn't lose my patience when Josh asked questions like, 'I know I can't pick it up, but can I scoop the ball along the ground with my hands?'

Dylan and I had to put together a training schedule for both teams, figure out which players should be on which team and then work out positions. It's exhausting! I don't know how coaches do it all year round.

I feel lucky because Indi's on my team and sorry for Dylan because he got lumped with Chelsea. But he didn't seem too fazed about it. He says that he's captain so she has to do what he says. I'm not sure. Since when has Chelsea ever done what she's supposed to?

It's been weird having Dylan as my rival. We've both been secretly working on our game plans. I know Dylan was trying to read over my shoulder at lunchtime the other day when I was working out some strategies for my two best players, Lily and Max.

'Hey!' I said, pulling the paper away as I felt Dylan lean over to 'put something in the bin'! 'No snooping!'

'I'm not!' Dylan had cried, pretending to be offended.

'He totally was,' Indi said matter-of-factly. 'But you can't talk, Sam. I saw you peeking at Dylan's game plan yesterday.'

Dylan's eyes bugged out of his head. '*What?!*'

'Gotta stay on the ball, Dylan,' I said, shrugging.

And on top of all that, I've been helping Indi learn her lines for the play whenever I can. She has SO MANY. There's no way I'd be able to remember all those words, but Indi is all over it.

'It's easy,' she says. 'It's just like learning the words to a song but they're spoken instead of sung.'

But even with all that going on, right now I need to focus on the Knights game this week. I glance up at the poster of David Beckham on my wall and think that if someone had told me a few months ago that I'd be playing in a soccer team with a shot at the finals, I'd have thought that they were crazy.

'Isn't that right, David?' I say, just as Indi walks back into the room.

'Ummm … were you talking to your poster?'

'Maybe.' I grin.

'Cool!' she says, flopping onto the bed. 'So, what's for dinner?'

CHAPTER FIFTEEN

THE VIPERS' HOME GROUND
SATURDAY
2.35 pm

'SAM! Get your head in the game!' Ted says. 'Where are you today?'

Oh no. Ted is in the middle of his half-time pep talk and here I am gazing off into the distance.

'Sorry, Ted,' I say.

'Did you hear what I said?' Ted asks, frowning at me from under his red cap.

I swallow nervously. I have no idea what he said. 'Um, I think you ...'

Ted sighs. 'I said you're in midfield so remember to keep the triangle formation.'

'Yep, got it coach,' I say.

'You okay?' Dylan asks as we walk back out onto the pitch.

'Yeah, I was just thinking about the school teams and ... we have to give them names and ...'

'Sam!' Dylan says, snapping his fingers in front of my face. 'Not now. All you have to think about is this game we're playing, right now. It's *imperative* that you focus, okay?'

'Okay, I will.'

It's half-time in our game against the Vipers and the score is 1–1, so the stakes are high. As the game starts again, I do exactly what Dylan told me to do and a few minutes later the ball is in my possession. Now all I need to think about is how I'm going to dodge around the Vipers player who is a whole head taller than me, and keeps trying to block every chance I have to run down the pitch with the ball.

I manage to get in a short pass to Noah, who moves straight into an open space and slices a pass to Dylan. He controls it, sprints towards our goal and kicks. It soars past the goalie's outstretched gloves and hits the back of the net.

'*YES!*' I shout.

Our supporters go crazy, screaming and shouting, '*GO KNIGHTS!*'

I run towards him for a high-five, and hear Indi shout out, 'Nailed it, Dylan!' Out of the corner of my eye I see both Dylan's family and mine all jumping up and down on the sidelines.

But five minutes later, the tall Vipers player scores an easy goal off the back of a throw-in and a subdued hush falls over our supporters. Chelsea did her best to intercept the throw-in, but the tall girl was too fast. She took the ball and weaved it around our players and surged down the middle of the pitch and booted it straight past Toby's gloves into the net.

Now the score is 2–2.

If the Vipers get another goal, it's all over for us in this competition. We need to stay in position and keep possession of the ball as much as possible to get it down to our goal and away from theirs. But it's not going to be easy. The Vipers are fast and their passing skills are outstanding.

'Remember your formation, Knights!' Ted yells from the sidelines. 'Stay in your positions!'

The Knights take the kick-off, but before we know what's happening, the Vipers have got the ball back in their goal area and their striker is lining up for a shot. Luckily, Toby is ready for it and knocks it away in time. I can almost hear our supporters breathing a huge sigh of relief.

Toby returns the ball to centre with a massive kick to Cooper, who snaps it across to Ky. Ky kicks the ball to me and I run with it for a bit before I feel a Vipers player bearing down on me. Chelsea is open and calling for the ball, so I slice a pass to her. She runs straight down the middle of the pitch towards the goal, controlling the ball with her feet the whole time. One of the Vipers players tries to intercept but Noah blocks him, giving Chelsea the chance to sprint free. She keeps her eyes on the net, and I watch as she pulls her foot back and kicks. The Vipers goalie reaches for it, but the ball shoots past him and straight into the left corner of the net.

GOAL!

I don't believe it!

We all run towards her, and Chelsea beams with pride and happiness as we slap her back and high-five each other.

'Great work, Chelsea!' Ted yells, taking off his cap and waving it in the air.

The ref blows his whistle to signal the end of the game. We've won, 2–3!

Without thinking, I run down the middle of the pitch, throw my body into a cartwheel, flip over backwards in the air and land squarely on my feet.

'Woooo-hoooooo!' A huge cheer goes up from the crowd.

'Fantastic work, team,' Ted says as we all jog off the pitch after shaking hands with our opposition. 'You totally deserved that win. You were focused and stayed in formation.'

'Sorry about before,' I say quietly to Ted as everyone walks over to collect their water bottles.

'No worries,' Ted grins. 'Just make sure you bring your full attention to the game next week. It's even more important than today's match.'

'I will,' I nod. 'Promise.'

And that's when it hits me. Next week is going to be huge! School Sports Day, Mum and Dad's surprise party and my big game with the Knights are all within three days of each other.

I'm excited and exhausted just thinking about it!

CHAPTER SIXTEEN

MY SCHOOL
THURSDAY
9.05 am

Indi, Dylan and I rock up to school on
Thursday morning to find the whole place
buzzing with excitement. Banners and
balloons in our school colours of green
and yellow hang off the main building,
someone has wrapped green and yellow
streamers around the basketball and netball

goal posts and pop music blares from a speaker in front of the grass steps. A bunch of preppies are dancing to the music.

Sports Day is finally here!

First, Miss McLeish makes a speech to kick things off and officially open the day, while the rest of the teachers walk around with megaphones, making sure everyone knows where they need to be at certain times.

The soccer match is the last event of the day, so Dylan, Indi and I are free to roam all over the school watching the other games and events. A lot of parents have come to watch their kids and my mum and dad have said they'll be here to watch us play soccer later.

First up are the netball games.
Dylan, Indi and I stand on the sidelines
with the rest of the kids who aren't
playing, and wave our yellow and green
banners, clapping and cheering every
time someone gets a goal. Chelsea and
Nikita are both playing, and when
Chelsea scores three goals in a row,
I shout, '*ONYA CHELSEA*!' She looks
over and rolls her eyes, but I can tell
she's chuffed.

The sack races are hilarious, especially
when Aalia Dhruv accidentally bumps
Charlie Mackavitch out of the way at the
last turn and hops her way to victory in
front of a roaring crowd. I'm pretty sure
I catch Mr Morton smiling, too.

Finally, it's time for the soccer match. I can almost feel the excitement zapping around me as teachers, parents and students gather behind the music room to watch our school's newest addition to Sports Day.

Indi loves her yellow goalie gear and I can't help but giggle every time she smashes her huge goalie gloves together and jumps up and down on the spot. Indi has been so busy with *Peter Pan* rehearsals that she's only made it to a couple of our lunchtime training sessions, but she reckons she's watched Dylan and I play enough times to know what to do.

'Who knows,' she laughs as we walk out to play the first half, 'I might even join the Knights next season!'

Turns out that playing soccer with a school team where half the kids have never played before is TOTALLY different to playing with the Knights. A lot of them have no idea what they're doing, and that includes the referee, who is Miss McLeish. When Max, one of Dylan's players, goes offside three times in a row and Miss McLeish doesn't pick him up on it, I can feel my temper starting to rise.

What's the point in playing at all if people aren't going to learn the rules properly, I think to myself when Max scores an easy goal.

I'm just about to walk over and say something to Miss McLeish when I catch myself and stop. What is *wrong* with me? This isn't a serious competition.

It's Sports Day. It's supposed to be fun! Who cares if Max goes offside and scores a goal, or if Josh accidentally picks up the ball with his hands? I wanted soccer to be included in Sports Day so everyone could see how much fun it is, not so I could prove to everyone what a soccer expert I am. Right then and there I decide that I'm going to enjoy myself and not worry so much about the rules, or who wins or loses. It's okay that not everybody feels the same way about soccer as I do. I'm going to have a good time.

And you know what? It's the BEST decision I could have made.

I start having so much fun that at one point I have to stop running because

I'm laughing so hard at the sight of Indi practising her handstands in front of the goal because the ball is so far down the other end.

Lily Hallington is a total natural (no surprises there!) and I make a mental note to try and talk her into joining the Knights next season. Even Chelsea has a hard time getting the ball out from under her as Lily bolts down the pitch, easily controlling it with her feet and dodging around anyone who comes at her. She spots me running alongside her, about twenty metres away, and does an impressive side kick, slicing the ball straight towards me. I trap it under my foot and take it straight down to our goal where I shoot and score our team's first goal.

My whole team and everyone watching goes crazy, and Indi does three cartwheels in a row to celebrate. Even Mr Morton gets swept up in the excitement, waving his yellow and green pom poms around and doing the loudest finger whistle I've ever heard.

As promised, Ted has come along to watch and cheer us on. I can see him standing with mine and Dylan's mums, and they all seem to be having just as much fun off the pitch as we're having on it.

At one point, two girls who have never played before are trying to get the ball off each other and end up falling on the ground, laughing like maniacs. It's so funny that

I can't help laughing, too. But Chelsea is furious.

'Get up!' she shouts at them. 'This isn't a joke!'

But when Indi blocks Chelsea's shot at goal, it's hands down the best moment of the whole day. Everyone goes wild and I immediately launch into a backflip before running towards my best friend, jumping in her arms and knocking her to the ground.

Chelsea gets her own back when she manages to get the ball past Indi and into the net just as Miss McLeish blows the whistle to end the game. Dylan's team have won 2–1 and I'm so happy for him that I'm not even that upset about losing.

The most important thing is knowing that this soccer match has been a winner. Everyone has had so much fun and knowing that we made this happen is the best feeling in the world.

Half an hour later, the whole school is gathered in front of the main school building as Miss McLeish hands out the awards and ribbons for the day.

When she gets to soccer, I cheer louder than anyone as she calls Dylan's team up to receive their ribbons. But I get the shock of my life when I suddenly hear my name booming through the speaker beside her.

'Sam Kerr, can you come up here please?' Miss McLeish says into the microphone.

Many hands clap me on the back as I walk up to the lectern in a daze. All I can think is, *Why is she calling me up? We didn't win.*

When I make it to the front, Miss McLeish holds out a small gold trophy to me.

'This is for you, Sam,' Miss McLeish says, and I look down to see the words 'Outstanding Team Player and Organiser' engraved on the front. I'm blushing so hard that I must look like a traffic light in my yellow and green uniform.

'As it says on here, this award is for being an "Outstanding Team Player and Organiser",' Miss McLeish says into the microphone. 'You have shown exemplary school spirit over the past few weeks,

which is exactly what a day like this is all about. Congratulations, Sam!'

The whole school goes crazy, including Dylan and Indi who are jumping up and down and screaming their lungs out. Mum and Dad are right up the back, cheering too, and I'm pretty sure I even see Mum wipe away a tear.

'Thank you,' I say shyly.

'Okay, everyone, that's it for this year's Sports Day!' Miss McLeish says into the microphone. 'Thank you all for such a fabulous effort!'

Miss McLeish switches the microphone off and turns to me with a sheepish grin.

'I loved refereeing today,' she says, 'but I'm sorry if I got a few things wrong!'

'No problem!' I say. 'Thanks so much again for letting us play. It was the best!'

'Thank YOU, Sam,' Miss McLeish says warmly. 'I think soccer might have more than a few new fans after today.'

Just then, I spot Indi, still in her goalie gear, throwing the soccer ball up in the air and trying to head it to a giggling Dylan.

'You know what?' I grin up at Miss McLeish. 'I think you might be right.'

CHAPTER SEVENTEEN

MY HOUSE
FRIDAY
6.30 pm

'HAPPY ANNIVERSARY!' everyone shouts as Mum and Dad walk through the front door, a beaming Daniel following behind them.

'Oh, my goodness!' Mum cries, her eyes already filling with tears.

My parents look so stunned at the sight of fifty of their closest family and friends standing in their lounge room that I worry for a second that they might both pass out right there in the doorway.

'Well, this is ... I mean ... what the ...?' Dad stammers, looking like there are a few tears pooling in his own eyes.

Maddi, Levi and I run over and throw our arms around them.

'Were you surprised?' Maddi asks.

'You should have seen your faces!' Levi laughs.

'Do you like the balloon arch?' I ask.

Mum and Dad both laugh and pull us all in for a group family hug.

'I can't believe you organised all this!' Mum says, kissing me on the head. 'Thank you so much!'

'Best kids ever,' Dad says, ruffling each of our heads in turn then smiling at their guests who are watching us all with huge smiles on their faces. 'G'day everyone! What a fantastic surprise!'

As Mum and Dad move away to greet their friends, the four of us stay huddled together, feeling pretty chuffed with ourselves.

The Kerr lounge room is almost unrecognisable. It's completely decked out in red and gold streamers; there's a red, silver and gold balloon arch in the corner and we've hung a huge banner along the wall that reads, 'HAPPY ANNIVERSARY ROXANNE AND ROGER!'

Footy-shaped lights are strung across the roof and windows (it took AGES to hang them up there!) and we've put up a large photo board showing images from Mum and Dad's lives over the past twenty-five years.

Everyone from Dad's football club is here, as well as Mum's friends from work. My Aunt Sandra and cousin, Lily, her new husband, Richard, and so many other cousins, uncles and aunties, are here too, all to celebrate my awesome Mum and Dad.

'Come on,' says Maddi, 'let's put some music on and get the food out!'

'I'll heat up the sausage rolls!' Levi says, dashing off to the kitchen.

'Don't you dare eat any!' Maddi says, running after him.

'I'll see if anyone needs a drink,' Daniel says. 'You want a Coke, Sam?'

'Yes, please,' I say.

'Hey, Sammy!'

I turn to see my Aunt Sandra beaming at me, a cocktail in her hand. 'Maddi says the decorations were your idea!' she says. 'They look fabulous! With talent like this, you could end up being Fremantle's biggest Party Planner!'

The idea is so ridiculous that I almost choke on the massive salt and vinegar chip I've just shoved in my mouth.

'Yeah-nah,' I say, once I've recovered. 'Reckon I'll stick with sport instead.'

I'm still buzzing from the thrill of Sports Day yesterday, and now I have tomorrow's big match to look forward to as well. We beat the All-Stars last time we played them, so now we just have to do it again so we can get into the finals.

My mind begins to wander to tomorrow's game, but I quickly bring it back to the present. This party is too special, and we've worked too hard for me not to enjoy it. I put the Knights match out of my mind and head into the kitchen to hang out with my family.

CHAPTER EIGHTEEN

THE KNIGHTS' HOME GROUND
SATURDAY
2.05 pm

'This isn't going to be an easy game,'
Ted says during warm-up the next day.
'They've got three new players,' he
continues, 'and they're all fast and
tall so I need everyone to bring their
A game today. It's going to be a tough
match.'

He's not wrong.

When the All-Stars score a goal two minutes in, it's a shock to everyone, including the All-Stars themselves. They look a bit dazed even as they shout and high-five one another.

I've never seen so many supporters as there are here today. Every single one of our families have come to watch us play on the Bruce Lee Oval today. Even Chelsea's family is here. But everyone is a bit on edge, too. We know that this is our last shot at the finals. If we lose today, there will be no more soccer for the Knights this season. The stakes are high and there's a nervous buzz in the air.

And that All-Stars goal was exactly what I needed to spur me on.

I am NOT going to let us miss out on making those finals, I think as we jog back to our positions. The rest of my team must feel the same sense of determination because from the moment the ref blows her whistle, everyone is fired up and raring to go.

Toby takes possession from the kick-off. He slices a pass to Liam, who takes it and easily weaves around his opponent to bolt away down the pitch, before passing to Dylan. Ky is in an open space and calls for the ball. Dylan boots it to Ky, just before an All-Stars player can intercept.

'KY!' I'm totally open so I call for the ball, then pass it to Archie straight away.

My hopes start to rise as I watch us all playing as a team, but when Chelsea calls for the ball, I can't help but worry. She is definitely too far out to have a shot at goal. Is she going to take a chance on losing possession, or will she pass it to someone with a better shot?

'CHELSEA!' James calls. He's right near goal and has the best chance at scoring. I hold my breath as Chelsea hesitates for a second, then dodges around an All-Stars player to get the ball to James.

Just before the ball is swept out from under his foot, James kicks it straight into the back corner of the net and ...

GOAL!

We all run over to slap James on the back, and as Chelsea runs up to the group, I turn and give her a grin and a thumbs up.

'Nice passing!' I say excitedly. 'Great work, Chels.'

She looks taken aback for a second, then shrugs it off and gives me a half-grin. 'Thanks,' she says gruffly.

At half-time, the score is still 1–1 and Ted is the most nervous I've ever seen him. Beads of sweat drip down the side of his face and he keeps taking off his cap and wiping his brow with the back of his hand.

'Keep talking to each other,' he says. 'You need to take control of this game as a team, got it?'

'Yes coach!' we all chime.

'You guys know what you're doing out there, so you just need to play towards your strengths,' he continues. 'Keep putting pressure on the opposition. It forces them to work harder. We want to tire them out. And when they have the ball, I want every single one of you to play defence.'

A few months ago, I would have had no idea what Ted was talking about, but now it's all crystal clear to me what he needs us to do.

'Ky, I think you can afford to be a bit more aggressive when you're playing defence,' he says, turning to address each of us in turn. 'Cooper, open up the space, don't crowd in on the action. Dylan, remember to use your options on the wings. Sam, if you're open, I want you to run straight for a shot at goal instead of passing, okay?'

'Yep, got it,' I say.

I sprint out onto the pitch, itching to get back out there and win this game!

The second half is even tougher than the first, and way more stressful. The All-Stars have three different shots at goal, but Liam is on fire and knocks away every attempt. It's so nerve wracking because as much as we try to keep the ball down our end, it spends way more time down the All-Stars' end of the pitch. I can almost feel the tension and nerves coming off our supporters on the sidelines.

After yet another missed goal by the All-Stars, and with only a few minutes left in the game, Dylan throws the ball in to Archie who is immediately swamped by All-Stars players. Ky does exactly what Ted told him to and gets right in there, somehow emerging from the pack with the ball at his feet. He slices a quick short pass to Chelsea, who runs down the pitch, looking around for someone to pass it to. I'm in an open space, so I call out to her as she heads straight down the middle. 'CHELSEA!'

I see her hesitate for just a millisecond before passing to me, and I trap it under my foot to control it. Out of nowhere, the tall girl is on me like she's my new bestie

and sweeps the ball out from under my
foot with a quick scissor step.

Oh no you don't, I think, chasing after her.

'That's it!' Ted shouts. 'Get after her,
Sam!'

As I'm running alongside this tall
fast girl, I suddenly know exactly what I
need to do. When the moment is right,
I pounce, swiping the ball away from her
with my left foot and she stares at me
in shock. I can't help feeling a tiny bit
smug. It's one of the huge perks of being
ambidextrous, tricking the opposition
when I use the foot they were never
expecting.

With the ball back in my possession,
I'm determined not to lose this chance.

I'm going to take the ball all the way to our goal and boot it into that net with every bit of strength I have. There's no one on me so I do exactly what Ted told me to do at half-time. Instead of passing, I run straight towards goal and, when I'm in range, pull my right foot back and kick it as hard as I can. The goalie tries to grab it, but the ball flies past him and straight into the right corner of the net.

GOAL!

The ref blows her whistle to signal the end of the game and the Knights supporters go wild with cheering, clapping, whistling and woo-hooing. Dylan's mum and dad start shouting and jumping up and down alongside Indi and my family. I laugh and wave to them all, and when Dad blows me a kiss, I almost burst into happy tears right there and then.

We did it! We made the finals!

I run towards my teammates and straight into their waiting huddle.

'SAM! BACKFLIP! BACKFLIP! BACKFLIP!'

I turn around to see my family and friends all beaming and chanting at me.

'Go on,' Chelsea says, grinning and rolling her eyes. 'Gotta give your fans what they want!'

As I break away from my teammates and prepare to do the best backflip of my life, I turn back to Chelsea and grin.

'*OUR* fans,' I say. 'We're a team. The best team in the WHOLE WORLD!'

And in that moment, I truly believe that we are.

ABOUT SAM KERR

Sam Kerr is the captain of the Australian women's national soccer team — the Matildas — and a leading goal scorer for Chelsea in the English FA Women's Super League. She burst onto the W-League scene as a fifteen-year-old playing with Perth Glory. In 2016, she played for the Matildas at the Olympics in Brazil, and she was the top goal scorer in the 2017 Tournament of Nations. Since joining Chelsea in 2019, Sam has positioned herself as one of the best female strikers in the world. She was named 2018 Young Australian of the Year. In 2021, Sam became the Matildas' all-time top goal scorer at the Tokyo Olympics, and she is currently preparing for the FIFA Women's World Cup to be held in Australia and New Zealand in 2023.

ABOUT FIONA HARRIS

Fiona Harris is an Australian actor and author who has written numerous children's book series including the *Super Moopers, Trolls* and *Miraculous*. This is her third book in the Sam Kerr *Kicking Goals* series. Fiona has also written a picture book with AFL star Marcus Bontompelli and is the author of two adult fiction books, *The Drop-off* and *The Pick-up*, both adapted from her internationally award-winning comedy web series, *The Drop Off*. Fiona has co-written and starred in TV sketch comedy shows including, *SkitHouse* (Channel 10), *Flipside* (ABC TV) and *Comedy Inc – The Late Shift* (Channel 9) and was head scriptwriter on ABC3 TV's *Prank Patrol*. For more information on Fiona Harris please visit fionaharris.com.

COMING SOON!

Available in print, eBook and eAudio
in November 2022

Read on for a sneak peek!

CHAPTER ONE

MY HOUSE
SATURDAY
5.30 pm

'Oh, look!' Maddi says, pointing out the window. 'They must be our new neighbours!'

As Dad turns into our driveway, we all turn to look at the family standing on the front lawn of the house next door. The Harris family moved out a few months ago and a SOLD sign went up out the front a few weeks later. We've been waiting to find out who our new neighbours will be and there they are! A mum, a dad and two boys – one who looks my age and the other a few years younger.

'Let's go and say hello,' Mum says, unclipping her seatbelt.

'But I need to have a shower!' I groan.

'You can say that again,' Maddi says, screwing up her nose.

I'm not smelling my best right now. We went straight from today's game against the All-Stars to Ted's house for a BBQ to celebrate our epic win in the semi-finals, so yeah, Maddi's right.

'You can say hello first, Sam,' Mum says firmly. 'Then you can have a shower.'

'Do we have to go over, too?' Levi grumbles.

'Yes, you do,' Dad says. 'It's the neighbourly thing to do.'

We all step out of the car to walk across the driveway that separates our two houses and Mum lifts her hand to wave as we approach them.

'Hello,' she chirps in a friendly voice. 'You must be our new neighbours!'

The mum smiles. 'Oh yes, hello!' she says.

The mum is wearing khaki shorts and a white singlet and has a nice smiley face, but the dad just gives us the kind of tight smile you'd give a stranger on the bus.

'I'm Roxanne,' Mum says, 'this is my

husband, Roger, and our kids, Sam, Levi and Madi.'

'Lovely to meet you all,' the mum says. 'I'm Lucy, this is my husband, Spike, and our boys, Jake and Will.'

The boys are both small and have messy brown hair that flops down over their eyes. The small one keeps pushing it back behind his ear, but it keeps flopping forward onto his face again.

'They're starting at the school down the road on Monday,' Lucy continues. 'Will is in grade four, and Jake in grade six.'

'That's where Sam goes,' Dad says, jerking his head at me. 'She's in grade six, too.'

'Oh, that's nice,' Lucy says. 'We just moved from Melbourne and the boys don't know anyone here yet.'

'It's a good school,' I say, smiling at Jake. 'I can show you around on Monday if you want?'

'Okay, thanks,' Jake says with a grin.

'I'm in grade four,' Will says loudly. 'I'm going there, too.'

I smile at him. 'I can show you around too, Will.'

'Okay,' he shrugs. 'Cool.'

'Do you play soccer, Sam?' Lucy asks, nodding at my uniform.

'Yep,' I say. 'With the Knights. Our home ground is at Bruce Lee Oval, just down the road.'

'Her team got into the finals today,' Maddi says. 'It looked like it was going to be a draw but then Sam did her ambidextrous feet thing and tricked the opposition. She kicked the winning goal!'

I stare at Maddi in amazement. I had no idea she was paying that much attention to the game. I thought she was just doing the 'good sister' thing by coming to watch. Maddi isn't exactly what you'd call a soccer expert. I'm not the only one who's shocked either. Levi makes a sound that's halfway between a snort and a laugh, and Dad arches one eyebrow at Mum.

'What?' Maddi says, seeing our expressions. 'I do watch the game you know! It was exciting!'

It was SO exciting. The game was hours ago but the buzz still hasn't worn off. We all played so hard to get into the finals and we did it!

Afterwards at Ted's we couldn't stop talking about the match. We replayed all our favourite moments as we sat around the outdoor table cramming Cheezels and potato chips into our mouths.

'How about when Chelsea dodged around that All-Stars player and sliced the ball to James?' Archie said.

'Oh yeah, that was wicked!' Toby agreed.

'And that goal, James!' Ky crowed. 'BOOM! Straight into the back corner!'

'Liam, you were on fire, today!'
I added.

'But your goal was the best, Sam!'
Cooper said.

I'm not gonna lie ... it *was* an epic
goal. But it was definitely a team effort.
Chelsea passed the ball to me right at the
perfect moment, which is the only reason
I could make the shot. I still can't believe
that we're going to be playing in the
finals!

'Congratulations,' Spike says now.
'That's fantastic!'

It's the first time Jake's dad has opened
his mouth so I'm guessing he's a soccer fan.

'It was a great game,' Dad says proudly,
putting his arm around my shoulders.

'We're more of an AFL family, but Sam here might just turn us around.'

'Us too!' Jake cries. 'We barrack for the West Coast Eagles.'

'You're kidding!' Mum laughs. 'My son plays for the Eagles.'

'No WAY!' Jake's eyes almost pop out of his head. 'Who?'

'Daniel Kerr,' Dad says.

Spike looks like he might explode with excitement. 'Oh, he's sensational!'

As the adults start talking football, Levi and Madi make a sneaky getaway back across the driveway and into our house.

Will looks up at me with eyes as big as saucers. 'Does your brother really play for West Coast?' he asks.

'Yep,' I say. 'Sure does.'

'But you don't play footy,' Will says, frowning at my uniform.

'No, but I still love AFL,' I grin.

'I don't know anything about soccer,' Jake says, frowning. 'Is it fun?'

'Heaps of fun,' I say. 'I only started playing this year, but I love it. I can teach you a bit about it if you like?'

'Cool!' Jake's expression brightens. 'Thanks!'

When I first started playing soccer, I didn't know anything about it either. There are so many rules to learn, like 'Offside' and 'Penalty Kicks' and 'Fouls', and it took ages to figure it all out. Now I can't imagine not understanding the game.

'Can we go inside now?' Will says,

looking up at Jake. 'You promised you'd help me set up my Lego table.'

'Yeah, okay,' Jake says. 'In a minute.'

'It's okay, I have to go get cleaned up,' I say, pulling at my dirty jersey. 'See you on Monday!'

'Come on, Jake!' Will says, tugging at Jake's sleeve.

'I'm coming,' Jake says, turning to go. 'See ya, Sam.'

Maybe I'll introduce Jake to Dylan and Indi on Monday morning, I think as I walk away. I reckon they'll like him. He seems like a good kid and I might even have someone else to kick the ball around with in the off season.

A someone who lives right next door!